This book belongs to

....

Written by Rosie Greening.
Illustrated by Stuart Lynch.

We are the grOOvicOrns!

ROSIE GREENING ★ STUART LYNCH

make
believe
ideas

Everyone **loves** unicorns. They always make a fuss.
But you know who **should** be famous?

but they make
amazing
slides!

Unicorns sign hoofprints,

My Unicorn Scrapbook

To Rabbit,

Love Glitter

Show-off.

and they grant your WiSheS, too.

HAPPY BIRTHDAY

We don't have
magic powers,

but we still make **dreams** come true!

Buckinghorn Palace

We have **MULTICOLORED** tents

All WELCOME

The unicorns
**bring
sunshine**
everywhere
they go.

The sun is **super boring.**
You know what's better?
SNOW!

The unicorns are bigheads –
they **SHOW OFF** all day long.

Glow 'n' go
hoof polish

Eau de
Cotton
Candy

*The stunning
new scent*

Who would
want to smell
like cotton candy?

The snooty
unicorns,
that's who!

They **never** want to play with us, and —

HEY!

You've got it wrong.

Mane-gain!

Grow luscious locks in minutes

They're not THAT bad . . .

It's **hard** to be a **unicorn** – we have a **lot** to do.

There's **never** any time to play. We wish we were like **YOU!**

To Do
Make rainbow
*
Grant wish
*
Rainbow school
*
Hoofprint signing
*
Mane maintenance
*
Polish hooves
*
Attend premiere

Everyone is different,
but **special** in their way.

So let's **learn** from one another
and have more **fun** every day!